THE HAIR SALON

AN EROTIC ADVENTURE

VICTORIA RUSH

VOLUME 43

JADE'S EROTIC ADVENTURES - BOOK 43

COPYRIGHT

For the uninhibited...

WANT TO AMP UP YOUR SEX LIFE?

Sign up for my newsletter to receive more free books and other steamy stuff. Discover a hundred different ways to wet your whistle!

Victoria Rush Erotica

1

___

I never particularly enjoyed having my hair colored professionally. Besides the painstakingly long process of having my strands individually dyed and wrapped in ugly foils, I had to sit in an uncomfortable chair for two hours smelling the awful stench of the coloring chemicals. At least I had my phone to keep me distracted for part of the time, but there's only so many games of Candy Crush you can play before you literally feel like pulling your hair out.

After my last treatment, I'd sworn off the idea of having it ever done again, but after seeing one of my favorite actresses at a televised awards ceremony in a pretty sun-bleached bob, I decided to give it one more try. I googled her red carpet photo, then took a screenshot on my phone and scheduled an appointment with my colorist. On the day of my appointment, the salon was busier than usual and I scrunched up my nose smelling the reek of chemicals permeating the room as three other women sat patiently in their chairs waiting for their color to set.

"Good morning, Jade," the salon owner Nikki said greeting me, motioning for me to take the last open chair when she finished with her last client. "It's been a while since you've been in for a coloring. What's the occasion?"

"Nothing special," I said, tapping my phone to pull up the photo I'd saved. "I just thought this new look Amanda Seyfried was sporting at the Golden Globes looked pretty glam, and I felt like a change."

"Mmm," Nikki said, nodding her head as she peered at my screen. "I also noticed her on the show last week. It's a spectacular cut, and that strawberry blonde color looks great on her."

"Do you think you can duplicate it?"

"Of course, but are you sure about the color? You've been a straight blonde for quite a while now, and I know how much you dislike the coloring process. It'll be difficult to match your natural color again without letting it grow out."

"What the hell," I said, looking at all the other women tied up in hair clips while they stared at their smartphones. "You only live once, right? No pain, no gain."

"That's *one* way of putting it," Nikki chuckled. "I'll try to make this as painless as possible. Hold tight while I mix the color for you. Can I borrow your phone to use the photo as a benchmark?"

"Of course," I said, giving her a wink as I handed over my phone. "Just don't drop it. The cost to replace it is even higher than your coloring fees."

"Not to worry," she chuckled. "I'm pretty sure my prices are lower than what Amanda Seyfried paid for her do."

While Nikki retreated to the rear of the store to prepare the treatment, I looked at the panel of mirrors lining the wall, scanning the faces of the other women getting their hair colored. Each of them looked bored out of their minds while they tapped their phone screens as they shifted uncomfortably in their salon chairs. When one of them looked up to catch my gaze, I smiled at her with a lopsided grin to convey my sympathy with her predicament.

Color? she mouthed the word, pointing to the mess atop her head.

I nodded and she shook her head with a frown, knowing what I was in for.

A few minutes later, Nikki returned, placing her mixing bowl and brushes on the table beside my chair.

"All set?" she said, peering at me in the mirror.

"As ready as I'll ever be," I said, gripping the armrests on my chair tightly.

"What *is* it about this process that you abhor so much, anyway?" she said, noticing my white knuckles.

"You mean besides the awful stench of the chemicals and having to stare at my ugly head all tied up in greasy knots and tangled hair clips for two hours?" I scoffed. "Nothing gives me more pleasure."

"Well, you don't exactly have to stare at *yourself* the whole time," she said, handing my phone back to me. "Surely you can find some *other* things to keep yourself amused while connected to our salon Wi-Fi. Maybe you can watch a movie of your favorite actress or search for your next hair style."

"Maybe," I said, shifting uncomfortably in the upright chair. "But I already spend way too much time staring at my computer screen all day long. It would be nice to have a *different* kind of distraction when I get out of the house."

"You mean besides the stimulating conversation with your favorite stylist?"

"You know how much I love getting caught up with you, Nikki," I smiled. "But getting my hair dyed isn't quite the same as getting it cut. After you put the color in, I'm pretty much left to my own devices for an hour and a half while you look after other clients."

"It's the nature of the beast," she nodded. "It takes that long for the dye to permeate your hair and properly set. I hazard to say that Amanda Seyfried had to sit in her salon's studio for more than two hours to create her new look."

"I know," I said, shaking my head apologetically. "The end result is normally worth the investment. It's just that the *rest* of the salon experience is actually quite stimulating and enjoyable. The shampoo and head massage you give me afterwards is practically worth the price of admission alone. It's too bad you couldn't find something equally enjoyable to keep me occupied the rest of the time."

"What did you have in mind?" Nikki said as she began to separate my hair with her comb and brush in the color paste. "I enjoy your head massage almost as much as you do, but if you wanted me to give you a *full-body* massage the entire time it takes for your color to set, I'd have to triple my rates to cover the overhead."

I paused, peering at Nikki in the mirror with a sly smile.

"Maybe you could find some *other* kind of way to massage me while you're busy tending to other clients' needs," I smiled. "With all the advances in modern technology, it shouldn't be too hard to upgrade this chair with some new enhancements..."

"Like one of those expensive massage chairs?" she said.

"I was thinking more like a *Sybian* massage chair," I grinned. "To stimulate some *other* parts of my body. That could definitely keep me amused for a little while."

"No way," Nikki said, suddenly cocking her head toward me in the mirror. "Are you *serious*? Right here in the *open*, in full display of the other customers?"

"It's not like they'd know any better," I smirked. "With me

covered in a long apron and all the other buzz of activity going on in the salon, they probably wouldn't even hear the sound of the vibrator."

Nikki paused for a moment while she looked at me in the mirror.

"You could always bring one of your *own* if you needed that kind of distraction."

"Possibly," I said. "But I'd still have to sneak it out of my purse and position it under my gown to hold it steady. It would be a lot more convenient if you had something built in to the chair that I could control from the armrests."

"You're actually serious about this, aren't you?" Nikki said, staring at me incredulously.

"Why not? Think about the competitive edge it could give you. It wouldn't take long for your place to become known not only for its cutting-edge hair styles, but also for its invigorating salon experience."

"That's assuming we don't get raided by the cops first for running an illicit massage parlor–"

"Except that *you* wouldn't be actually doing the massage," I said. "It would all be self-administered from the privacy of our own chairs, at our own discretion."

"What about the *rest* of my clientele?" Nikki said, still not convinced. "I'm not sure some of the older women would approve of such licentious activity..."

"You never know until you try," I smiled. "I'm guessing some of them might appreciate it more than you imagine. Besides, you don't have to tell everybody about the special features."

"Where do you come up with these crazy ideas?" she said, shaking her head.

"Remember I was telling you the last time I was in here about some of the amazing new sex toys coming onto the market? The only difference in this case is that your clientele would be enjoying them in a completely different setting."

"In full view of all the other customers?"

"They don't need to know what's going on in the privacy of someone else's chair. But if they *did*, that might only increase the excitement level all the more."

"Jesus, Jade," Nikki said, wrinkling her forehead. "I don't know..."

"Why don't you outfit *one* chair to start? And only tell your most trusting clients. If they object to the idea, you can always remove the feature. But I have a feeling this might up your game and dramatically increase your book of business. You might even be able to raise your already exorbitant fees."

"You have a wicked mind, you know that, right?" Nikki said, peering at me in the mirror with a raised eyebrow.

"So are you thinking of giving it a try?" I smirked.

"You've certainly piqued my interest," she smiled, rubbing her thighs together while she finished setting the foils in my hair. "If nothing else, I'll be able to use the chair to keep *myself* amused when things get quiet in the salon..."

2

———

After my hair coloring finished, I decided to forego the styling portion of my appointment, hoping Nikki would take my suggestion to heart and make some modifications before my next session. When I visited the studio two weeks later, my panties were already wet in anticipation of trying out the new upgrades.

"Hey beautiful," she said when I entered the salon. "Love your new color. Do you miss being a blonde?"

"I'm not feeling quite as *stupid*, that's for sure," I grinned.

"*Good* one," Nikki laughed. "But you can't fool me. I know all the brilliant ideas rolling around in that pretty head of yours, no matter how well you try to camouflage it."

"Speaking of, have you made any changes to your setup based on my suggestions?"

"Let's talk about it over by the sink," Nikki nodded. "Maybe I can get you warmed up with a nice wash and head massage."

"You're twisting my arm," I said. "You know that's the favorite part of my visit."

"Maybe not for much longer," she smiled, leading me to

the back of the studio toward the bank of sinks on the far wall.

"So?" I said, sitting in the chair opposite one of the sinks and tilting my head back into the curved depression to rest my neck. "I'm dying to know if you've made any upgrades!"

"*Possibly,*" Nikki teased, adjusting the water temperature and pointing the warm spray over my head. "You'll just have to wait until you get seated for your cut."

"Who needs a vibrating chair when I've got the next best thing standing right over top of me?" I purred, feeling the soft wash flowing over my scalp as Nikki massaged the shampoo into my hair.

"Oh?" she smiled, kneading my head firmly with the tips of her fingers. "You like to be *fingered* once in a while instead?"

"If it's by someone as pretty and sexy as you, absolutely."

"Maybe I should expand my repertoire by offering full-body washes to my customers as well?" she smirked.

"Don't get me started," I groaned, rolling my hips at the thought of Nikki directing the pulsating spray on my wet pussy. "I'm already worked up enough at the thought of you watching me getting stimulated while you do my hair."

"I have to admit, it's gotten *me* pretty damn excited at the thought also. I can't wait to give this thing a try."

"You mean I'll be the first?"

"If you don't count me," she smiled. "I mean I had to test it before offering it to my customers, right?"

"And?" I said, batting my eyelashes as the warm spray spilled down over my forehead. "Does it work?"

"If you consider three incredibly powerful orgasms in the space of ten minutes a success, then I suppose so."

"*Fuck,* Nikki," I panted. "You're going to get me off right here if you keep talking like that."

"Judging by the spreading wet spot in your jeans, it would appear so," she said, glancing at my crotch. "We better get you gowned up before somebody guesses what's going on."

"Ok, but can I take a rain check on the full-body wash? I've been fantasizing about getting you alone for myself since the first day I stepped foot in your salon."

"That can be arranged," Nikki smiled. "I have to admit I was thinking of *you* too while I was trying out the new chair."

"*Damn*, girl," I grunted while she rinsed off the last of the shampoo residue from my head. "Clean me up, I can't wait to try this out!"

Nikki tilted my head up over the sink then draped a dry towel over my head, rubbing my hair vigorously while she tossed my head from side to side.

"Holy shit," I said, leaning forward and panting as she removed the towel and held out her hand to help me up from the chair. "Talk about *rubbing* one out. Nobody quite gives head like you do, Nikki."

"I'll take that as a compliment," she said, leading me over to the styling chair furthest from the front window.

When I approached the chair, I noticed a small triangle-shaped bump in the middle of the seat and four new buttons embedded in the right armrest. One was colored green and another red, with the other two simply marked 'Up' and 'Down'.

"This looks interesting," I said, rolling my fingers over the bulge. "It's a little different than the *Sybian* chair I'm used to, but it looks promising."

"Well, I couldn't very well place a four-inch-long dildo in the middle of my chair without making it obvious what it was there for."

"How are you going to explain this slightly less obtrusive addition?"

"If anyone asks, I'll just tell them it's meant to show where they're supposed to sit and not move around while I'm cutting their hair. But something tells me there won't be too many complaints once they figure out what it's *really* there for."

"Strap me in, babe," I smiled. "I'm ready to take it for the first test ride."

I climbed onto the chair then spread my legs while pressing my hips forward until I felt the leading edge of the bump pushing into my slit.

"Very ingenious," I nodded approvingly. "The shape conforms perfectly with the Vee of my vulva."

"I thought it would provide more surface area to stimulate your entire crotch area," Nikki nodded, throwing a plastic gown over my chest and tying it gently behind my neck.

"Brilliant," I said, already feeling my clit starting to tingle as I humped the tip with my hips. "Who did you get to set this up? It almost looks like a factory install."

"One of my clients has an electronics background. I took a couple of hours to install the equipment and re-thread the upholstery to hide the internal wiring. But it turned out better than I expected."

"So I'm not *really* the first one to give this a try then?" I grinned, peering at her with a raised eyebrow.

"You'll be the first one to try it in *public*," Nikki smiled.

"How does it work exactly?" I said, brushing my fingers over the controls.

"I wanted to make it as simple as possible to use," she said. "The green button turns the vibrator on and the red one turns it off. The other two buttons control the intensity of the unit, up and down."

"No controls for setting different *pulse* patterns?"

"This isn't exactly a state-of-the-art sex toy shop," she said. "But I have a feeling you'll find the basic controls more than adequate. Fire it up to give it a try."

I pressed the green button with my index finger then held my thumb down over the Up button for a few seconds, feeling the triangle-shaped hump beginning to vibrate between my legs.

"*Still* think you need multiple modes of operation to make it work?" Nikki smiled, noticing me jerk suddenly in the chair.

"Um..." I grunted, toggling the vibrator speed up a few notches. "I think this will do just fine."

"I *thought* you might like it," Nikki said, running her hands through my mane as she began to trim it with her scissors. "Do you think you'll be able to stay still while I cut your hair? I wouldn't want to poke an eye out or something while you're busy stimulating yourself."

"Or make me look like *Edward Scissorhands* by the time you're finished," I chuckled, feeling the pleasure beginning to spread around my hips.

"Exactly."

As Nikki began to style my hair, I closed my eyes, pressing my vulva harder against the bump in the chair. The harder I pushed against it, the further it pressed the seam of my jeans into my slit, heightening my pleasure even more.

"*Fuck*, Nikki," I panted. "This thing is perfectly designed to hit all the right places. I only wish I could enjoy it *naked* to experience its full potential."

"You might want to come with a skirt and no panties next

time," she said, cocking her head. "It's a million times better in the raw."

"I bet it is," I said, beginning to roll my hips under my apron. "But it still feels fucking awesome even with all my clothes on."

"Good enough to elevate my already exorbitant fees?" Nikki smiled.

"I'd pay *twice* your fee to sit in this thing for forty-five minutes while you do my hair. Something tells me you're about to become the most popular hair salon in town."

"We'll have to see about that," Nikki said. "I'm just happy to see my clients walking out of the place with a big grin on their faces."

"Ugnnn," I groaned, feeling the familiar pangs of a climax building up inside me. "Oh God, Nikki..."

"Let it go, baby," she purred, staring back at me in the mirror. "Let me watch you come while I hold your head. You've got a lovely red flush to match your new strawberry highlights."

As I stared back at Nikki feeling my pleasure rapidly rising, my mouth began to part and my eyes glazed over as I felt my orgasm washed over me. Trying not to reveal the pleasure I was feeling to the patrons on the other chairs beside me, I gripped the chair armrests tightly, trying to hold myself still while my body convulsed in powerful contractions.

"Damn, girl," Nikki purred, listening to me panting next to her while my head bobbed softly in her hands. "That's fucking hot. I nearly came *with* you watching you. This might be harder than I expected trying to concentrate on cutting your hair while you're enjoying yourself."

"This is *insane!*" I said, trying to catch my breath as my body jerked softly coming down from my climax. "There's something about doing this in full view of your other customers without them knowing what's going on that takes it to a whole new level."

"That, and not being able to squeal while you're coming under your apron?" Nikki smiled.

"Yeah," I nodded. "It reminds me of a dinner party I attended a while back where everybody watched me getting off while someone caressed me under the table. But in this case, it's even more stimulating trying to *hide* my pleasure."

"Don't let me stop you now," Nikki grinned. "I still need another twenty minutes or so to finish your cut. Knock yourself out while we continue pretending like nothing special is happening. You haven't even tried the maximum speed setting yet."

"I want to make it last," I said, turning the vibrator speed back down to build up to another climax. "You don't want me jumping out of my seat before you're finished, do you?"

"Go for it," she said. "I'm interested to see just how much you can stand while sitting still."

"You're on," I smiled, holding my finger over the Up button as the vibrator began to buzz harder against my clit.

"Mhhh," I grunted, pressing my cunt harder against the pointy bump. "I hope you've got plenty of disinfectant left over when I'm finished. Cause I'm pretty sure I'm going to leave a big wet spot on your chair by the time this is over."

"I hope so," Nikki said, smiling at me in the mirror as my face began to twist and distort trying to mask my rising plea-sure. "You might not be the *only* one needing to wear a skirt to your next hair appointment. This is turning me on so much watching you, I'm generating my *own* wet spot."

"Mmm," I groaned, gazing into Nikki's eyes as she peered back at me in the mirror. "I'm imagining it's your wet pussy rubbing up against me right now instead of this leather vibrator. I can't wait to get you into bed with your clothes off."

"Or under my sink?"

"However I can get you," I grunted while turning the vibrator speed up to the maximum setting. "I just want to feel your sexy body pressed up against me."

As I began to growl with a soft animal sound, some of the other women flanking me turned their heads to watch me in the mirror.

"You better keep your emotions in check lest you frighten the rest of my customers away," Nikki said, noticing the distraction of the other customers.

"I'm trying," I panted while gyrating my hips more rapidly under the fluttering apron. "But I don't think there's any turning back now."

"Damn, Jade," Nikki hissed over my shoulder. "This has to be the sexiest thing I've ever seen. I had no idea this would be so enjoyable for the *rest* of us when you proposed this idea."

"Maybe you should be giving me a *discount* instead of charging a premium?" I smiled, noticing the flush in my cheeks spreading down my neck as I bit my lip trying to suppress my rising pleasure.

"Maybe," Nikki panted beside me as she squeezed her legs together trying to stimulate her own aching clit. "This is sure better than any sexy movie or porn site I've ever watched."

"Oh Nikki," I grunted, gaping my mouth open as I approached another powerful climax.

"Yes, Jade," she groaned with her own sex flush beginning to roll over her cheeks. "You're going to make me come just watching you..."

"Oh *fuckkkk*," I hissed as another orgasm washed over me

while I began twitching and convulsing in my chair, gripping the armrests with white knuckles trying to hold myself steady.

By now, everybody in the room was staring at me squirming and moaning in my chair as the powerful vibrator between my legs continued to oscillate against my convulsing pussy. By the time my minute-long orgasm subsided, the only sound that could be heard in the room was the soft buzzing of the vibrator between my legs. While Nikki continued to cut my hair like nothing unusual was happening, another client sat in the salon chair next to me.

"What kind of cut would you like to today?" her stylist said to the woman.

"I'll have what *she's* having," the girl said, smiling at my flushed face.

3

———

After my previous visit to the hair salon, I could hardly wait for my next appointment. But this time, I came fully prepared, wearing a short skirt and no panties. I didn't want anything coming between me and the pointy vibrator embedded in Nikki's salon chair. When I entered the studio, she greeted me warmly at the front door, kissing me on both cheeks.

"You scheduled earlier than usual," she said.

"I was just getting itchy for another treatment," I smiled. "Ever since my last visit, I've been tingling all over awaiting another turn in your special chair."

"I see you came properly *prepared* this time," she said, peering at my high skirt. "Were you looking for a *coloring* or a cut? We usually recommend at least six weeks between dye treatments."

"Just a little trim will be fine this time," I said. "That should be more than enough time to satisfy my craving."

"Mmm," Nikki smiled. "I think we can get that looked after. Shall we start with the usual preliminaries?"

"Absolutely," I said. "I can't think of any better foreplay than another head massage from my favorite stylist."

Nikki led me to the bank of sinks on the back wall, and I assumed the wash position, tilting my head back as I spread my legs apart.

"So, what's been the response to your expanded suite of services?" I said, peering up at her while she adjusted the water temperature.

"Better than I expected. In fact, I've had to outfit the rest of the chairs based on unprecedented demand."

"Oh?" I said. "Your customers seem to be *enjoying* the upgrades?"

"That's a bit of an understatement," Nikki said, motioning toward the line of salon chairs filled with women. "I've never seen the place as busy as it's been these past few weeks."

"You don't think it's because of your reputation for superb hair styling?" I grinned.

"I'm pretty sure it's because of something *else*," she smiled, rubbing my head vigorously while she peered down at my skirt hiking up my bare thighs. "In fact, today's appointment is on me. If this keeps up, I might have to give you a free lifetime membership."

"Don't sweat it, babe," I moaned, enjoying her wet rubdown. I'm willing to pay your regular rate just to experience this exquisite head massage."

"I've made some new upgrades," Nikki smiled. "I have a feeling you're going to enjoy your *next* massage even more."

"Do tell," I said, flipping up my skirt to reveal my glistening pussy. "You're making me wet in a few *other* places imagining what enhancements you've made."

"I've been trying out a different kind of vibrator on one of the chairs. It's been in especially high demand since I had it installed. Unfortunately, it's booked up solid for three weeks, so you'll have to wait until your next visit to give it a try. But I can guarantee it'll be worth the wait."

"You've still got the regular vibrator installed on the other chairs?"

"Not to worry," she smiled, rinsing off the last of the shampoo residue into the sink. "You'll still be able to keep yourself properly amused while I cut your hair. Although you might find it even *more* interesting watching the reaction of the some of the other customers in the newly outfitted chairs."

"You've got that right," I said, peering over at the lineup of attractive women facing the mirror. "Nothing excites me more than watching a pretty girl get off, especially while she's stimulating herself."

"Well then, I've got a treat for you today. You'll be sitting in the chair next to the newly upgraded one. If you can't experience it directly, at least you can enjoy the next best thing."

Nikki led me over to the same chair I used last time, but before I sat down, I glanced at the empty seat next to me, noticing some new controls on the armrest and a strange slit in the middle of the fabric.

"What happened to the vibrator on the other chair?" I said.

"Oh it's still there," Nikki smiled. "It's just hiding out of sight beneath the upholstery. This one's got a new animated feature that lends an entirely new definition to the idea of yoni massage."

"You mean...?"

"Exactly," Nikki nodded. "I decided to take a page out of your Sybian playbook to elevate this massage experience to a whole new level."

"No fair!" I protested. "If you'd told me about that, I'd have waited a couple of extra weeks for my next appointment!"

"Who are you kidding?" Nikki smirked, throwing a gown over me while I hiked up my skirt and positioned my pussy over the triangle-shaped bulge. "I know you too well to know that you wouldn't be able to hold off any longer than absolutely necessary to get back into this seat. And neither could I. I've been fantasizing about watching you squirming in my chair ever since your last visit."

I turned my head, noticing a pretty brunette taking a seat in the chair next to me while her colorist prepared the treatment materials.

"Let's get this party started," I smiled. "I'm dying to take this thing for another ride."

As Nikki started to style my hair, I watched the pretty girl next to me making small talk with her colorist as she brushed in the dye. The girl hadn't placed her fingers on the armrest controls yet, and for a few minutes I wondered if she was even aware of the newly installed feature.

"What are you waiting for?" Nikki said, noticing me staring at the girl.

"Oh," I said, peering back up at her. "I was just wondering if you've told *all* of your customers about the new features."

"We didn't *have* to," she grinned. "Word got around pretty fast. We lost a few customers who were initially put off by the idea, but we more than made up for it with a rush of new customers who flocked to our studio to try it out. I think it's fair to say that *all* of our clients know about our expanded services at this point."

"And willing to try them *out*?" I said, peering at the new buttons on the adjacent chair.

"Take a look at the faces of the other women lining the wall. Do you notice anything different?"

I peered into the mirror, scanning the bank of chairs occupied by the other women whose hair was tied up in hair clips and coloring foil. Some of them had their eyes closed while they shifted quietly in their chairs, while others smiled at one another as their heads bobbed gently atop their shoulders. But virtually all of them had a flush on their faces as they panted softly. Everyone except the pretty brunette seated next to me, who still seemed preoccupied chatting with her colorist.

"Hmm," I nodded. "They don't look nearly as bored as usual. But not everybody seems to be enjoying themselves equally. Are you sure all of the chairs are outfitted the same way?"

"All but the one next to you. It's just that not everybody likes to take advantage of the feature while they're engaged with their stylist. Some prefer to enjoy the experience when they have a little more privacy."

"If you can call being lined up cheek-by-jowl in front of a salon-wide mirror *private*," I chuckled.

"At least they're all covered in a cape and nobody can see what's going on underneath it. Nobody knows for sure exactly who's doing what at any given time."

"Although it's not too hard to tell where each of them are in their arousal cycle," I grinned, watching one of the women at the far end parting her mouth as the flush on her face began to spread down her neck.

"It's pretty hard to hide it once you get to a certain point," Nikki nodded. "But most of the girls keep the vibration setting at a low level most of the time. You can only take the full intensity of the vibrator for so long."

"True," I said, watching another woman beginning to

jerk spastically in her chair as she slipped over the edge. "But that doesn't stop some of us from adjusting the levels to experience *multiple* orgasms depending on how long we have to sit in the chair."

"You mean like you did *last* time?" Nikki smiled.

"I had a little help watching *you* getting just as turned on watching me."

"I did," Nikki smiled. "But it's not quite the same as receiving direct stimulation to the targeted area."

"Speaking of..." I murmured, glancing over at the girl seated next to me. "Do you think we're going to see the pretty brunette getting a little workout before we're finished?"

"Give it a few more minutes," Nikki said, nodding toward the colorist as she picked up her materials to let the dye set. "This one's a little shy."

After her stylist left to look after other clients, the girl darted her eyes across the mirror and I glanced away so as not to make her feel scrutinized. Soon after, her hand wandered over her armrest controls and she groaned, sinking lower in her chair. Before long, her hips began to move rhythmically under her gown and her breathing beginning to escalate.

"What exactly did you *put* in that chair?" I whispered to Nikki, trying to keep my lips still so the girl didn't suspect I was spying on her.

"You'll just have to wait until your next visit to find out," Nikki smiled. "That is, if you remember to schedule your appointment before it's booked solid for another month.

"Nnngh," the girl began to moan as she closed her eyes, gripping her armrests more tightly with both hands.

"*Jesus*," I said, beginning to feel my juices pooling between my thighs.

I'd been so distracted watching the girl next to me, I hadn't even bothered to turn on my vibrator. I flicked the on switch and pressed my hips forward while I ramped up the speed, feeling the pointy tip sinking deep between my folds.

"Whatever it is," I panted, "it seems to be exciting her even more than mine. If there's such a thing as reincarnation, I want to come back as that salon chair."

"She's pretty fucking hot, that's for sure," Nikki chuckled next to me. "Enjoy it, baby. At least *one* of us will be able to get off watching the show."

As a deep flush began to roll over her face, the girl grunted more loudly while her apron fluttered rapidly from the action of her writhing hips.

"*Uh–uh-uh,*" she groaned, squeezing her eyelids tighter.

"*Fuck me,*" I grunted, becoming increasingly turned on watching her inch closer toward an orgasm.

"Soon enough, babe," Nikki purred, rubbing her mound against the side of my chair as she watched the girl's rising pleasure along with me. "You have no idea what you're in for next time."

I held my finger over the Up button on my armrest, adjusting the vibrator to its maximum speed while I moaned in tandem with the girl next to me. Just as I started to feel my own orgasm welling up inside me, she suddenly flung her eyelids open, staring at me in the mirror with wide eyes.

"Oh my God," she groaned, jerking her torso forcefully as her climax took hold of her.

"Fuckkk," I groaned with my own orgasm washing over me while we stared at each other twitching in our chairs.

Suddenly the entire room was filled with the sound of the rest of the women moaning and gasping while they all stared at the two of us cumming hard in our chairs. The pretty brunette never took her eyes off me as we gaped our mouths open together in mutual pleasure. Even Nikki grunted noisily beside me while she held onto the side of my chair for support as she ground her pussy into my armrest.

"Holy *fuck*," I muttered after we came down from our powerful climaxes. "I have *got* to try that thing out as soon as it's available. Preferably while it's still covered with that beauty's juices."

"I'll see if I can schedule it before you leave," Nikki smiled, straightening herself up trying to concentrate on finishing my hair.

4

———

The three weeks I had to wait for my next hair appointment couldn't pass by fast enough while I fantasized about trying out Nikki's newly upgraded salon chair. All I could think about was the pretty brunette twisting and squirming in her seat while she gripped her armrests with bear claws. Whatever Nikki had installed under her seat had caused her to have an incredibly strong orgasm while she convulsed in her chair for almost a full minute. When I entered the studio, my pussy was already dripping wet in anticipation as I tried to hide the rivers of juices running down the inside of my thighs under my short skirt.

"Hey beautiful," Nikki said, kissing me on my cheek as she pressed her breasts against mine in a tight hug. "Are you ready to try out my new chair this time?"

"Are you *kidding* me," I said, pulling her hand over my ass cheeks to feel my slick thighs. "I haven't been this wet since my first lesbian experience."

"Well, you're about to have an entirely *new* kind of girl-on-girl experience this time," she said.

"You mean while you rub me down under the sink?" I smiled.

"Well that's not exactly *new*, but with you already this worked up, maybe you'll enjoy it even more this time."

"*Do* me," I panted into her ear. "I want to feel you finger me until I squeal like a baby."

"You might get a bit lucky," she said, leading me by the hand to the back of the room. "We've got the sinks all to *ourselves* since the rest of my clients have been already prepped."

I lay my head in the depression in one of the sinks, and Nikki wasted no time spraying the pulsating water over my scalp as she lathered in the shampoo while I stared up at her.

"That feels *so* good," I purred, rolling my hips sexily. "I only wish you could be doing that to me a little bit lower."

"Except you've got no hair down there for me to wash," she smiled.

"Who needs hair," I said, hiking up my skirt to reveal my dripping pussy. "When you've got magical fingers like those?"

"I'd love to accommodate you," she said, glancing over at the line of customers occupying the full bank of styling chairs. "But I'm not sure we could get away with it in this open space. Although you might be able to slide your *own* hand under your skirt without being noticed while I give you a rub-down."

I quickly slipped my hand under my skirt, pressing two fingers into my hole as I peered up at Nikki.

"Fuck yes," I purred. "I'm going to get you to myself in this place one way or the other before long. I love getting off while you watch me, but I want to feel something other than a plastic vibrator rubbing up against me the next time you do my hair."

"Well then, today might be your lucky day," Nikki smiled, splashing the warm water softly over my forehead. "Because I've got something a little different in store for you while you get your hair styled."

"Oh?" I said, blinking my eyes as I spit the water playfully up toward her face. "Are you going to sit down with me on the chair and rub your pussy against mine?"

"Not this time," Nikki teased. "But I think what you'll experience will be as close to the real thing as you can get without someone actually being next to you."

"Fuck, Nikki," I panted while thrusting my fingers in and out of my sloshing pussy. "I don't know what I'm enjoying more, you massaging my head, or imagining what you've got waiting for me."

"You might want to save something for when you're in the *other* chair," she said, watching me rock my hips more rapidly approaching a climax. "I'd hate for you to waste a perfectly good orgasm when the *rest* of the girls could be enjoying it along with you."

"Okay," I said, pulling my fingers out of my dripping snatch while I licked my lips peering up at her. "But I'm only interested in *you* watching me come. I'm gonna fantasize it's you fucking me in the chair instead of a vibrator."

"Come on," Nikki said, spraying the warm water playfully over my face while she finished rinsing the conditioner out of my hair. "Let's go get you trimmed up while you experience a *different* kind of fingering."

As she led me over to the other salon chair, I felt my juices dripping all the way down to my calves in anticipation of what was in store. When we got to the chair, the other women sitting beside me smiled at me with lopsided grins knowing it was going to be something special.

"Anywhere in particular I should sit?" I said, glancing down at the slit in the seat.

"Sitting back is better than forward," Nikki smiled. "You can always adjust your position once the device engages."

"How does it *work* exactly?" I said, peering at the different controls on the armrest.

"The two-way arrow raises the vibrator up and down as far as you want. The up and down buttons work the same as before, adjusting the vibrator speed to the intensity you desire."

"It doesn't sound so different from the one I already used," I said with a puzzled look.

"Oh, this one is very different, I assure you," Nikki purred. "Feel free to activate it whenever you're ready."

I peered into the mirror, scanning the faces of the other women who were squirming in their chairs with soft flushes on their faces, then slowly pressed the top of the two-way arrow. Suddenly, a hard plastic dildo began rising out of the seat, pressing my folds apart as it entered my pussy.

"Huh!" I jumped up in my seat, not expecting the sudden intrusion.

"How's *that* for a realistic substitute?" Nikki smiled, peering at me in the mirror.

"You didn't tell me I'd be fucking a *male* surrogate this time," I panted, holding the button down as the phallus pressed deeper inside me.

"You're welcome to stop the device if it isn't working for you," Nikki kidded, parting my hair between her fingers while she started to snip it with her scissors.

"Are you *kidding* me?" I said, pressing my hips forward to

engulf the hard phallus in my hole. "I'm so fucking horny right now, I could fuck a billygoat."

"Do you feel anything *besides* the dildo?" Nikki said, snipping the scissors calmly over my head.

My eyes suddenly flung open when I felt a pair of prongs sliding over my clitoris as the dildo pressed further inside me.

"Holy *fuck*!" I hissed, tilting my hips forward to push the prongs harder against my tingling nub.

"Remind you of any *other* toys you've used lately?"

"It feels vaguely similar to my rabbit vibrator with the vibrating ears for stimulating my clit," I nodded.

"Exactly," Nikki grinned. "Except this one also thrusts *up and down* while you're sitting still. Hold your finger over the middle of the arrow to see what I mean."

I moved my finger to the center of the arrow and suddenly the dildo began pushing up and down like some kind of automated fucking machine.

"Oh my God!" I gasped, gripping the armrests more tightly.

"Now you know what the pretty brunette was experiencing the last time you were in here," Nikki said.

"Unghh," I groaned, feeling my whole body being pushed up and down from the action of the pumping dildo. "This is *way* better than a Sybian machine. It's almost like I'm being fucked by a real man!"

"Or a woman," Nikki smiled. "Nowadays, it can be arranged it either way."

"What do the up and down buttons control?" I grunted, feeling my pussy juices beginning to spread over the leather seat.

"They adjust the speed of the vibrating prongs," Nikki

said. "Give it a try. I think you'll find it takes the experience to a whole new level."

I pressed my finger over the Up button and suddenly the soft appendages on the base of the dildo began to flutter against the sides of my twitching clit.

"Mmfff," I groaned, pressing my pussy harder against the pumping dildo. "This is way better than a real cock. If only a man's penis was outfitted this way. They'd never have difficulty ever again making a woman come."

"I thought you'd like it," Nikki smiled, noticing the other women staring in the mirror watching me as they began to squirm more actively in their seats. "And from the look of it, so do the *rest* of my clients."

"Have most of them already given this one a turn?" I said.

"Yes," Nikki said, nodding while she met some of their gazes. "But I'm trying to spread the wealth around so everybody can give it a try."

"Why not outfit *all* of the chairs this way?"

"Like you said before, it's hard to cut a person's hair without making them look like Edward Scissorhands when they're hopping up and down in the chair this way. At least the *regular* vibrator keeps you relatively still in one place."

"I'll stop moving soon enough," I panted, feeling the familiar pangs of a powerful orgasm beginning to build up inside me. "I just need a few more seconds before I can tamp this thing back down."

"Knock yourself out, babe," Nikki smiled. "I'm happy to stop while you get your rocks off."

"Are you getting as excited as *I* am watching me getting fucked by this thing?"

"Not as much as I am imagining me fucking you *myself* the next time you're in here."

"Oh God, Nikki," I groaned. "You're going to make me come talking like that..."

"As if you need much help at this particular moment," she smiled, caressing my scalp with her fingers.

"Fuck, Nikki," I hissed. "I love feeling your hands on me. I'm going to come so hard..."

"Let it go, baby," Nikki said, digging her nails into my scalp. "Squirt your juices all over that big dildo while you imagine my fingers are rubbing your clit. Soon enough you'll feel my *whole* body pressed up against yours."

"Oh *fuck*!" I screamed out loud with my body tightening up as my pussy began clamping down on the thrusting dildo and I gushed all over the flapping prongs at the base of my clit.

As I shook in my seat with my apron fluttering from the action of my rocking hips, I watched in rising ecstasy while many of the other women lined up against the mirror came simultaneously, groaning along with me. For what seemed like an eternity, I rocked and rolled in my chair, held like a clamp by the hard piston pounding up and down inside me. I'd never felt such a powerful full-body experience being stimulated in so many places with so many people watching me come. When I finally stopped shaking, I paused the vibrator and slumped down in my seat, peering up at Nikki.

"I had no idea it was going to be this good when I suggested this idea to you a few weeks ago," I panted. "Who knew getting your hair done could be so much fun!"

5

After my experience on the thrusting dildo chair, I eagerly awaited my next appointment at the salon. As requested, Nikki scheduled me back-to-back behind the pretty brunette, who'd booked herself four weeks out. It took every ounce of my willpower not to visit the studio earlier hoping for a walk-on appointment or a cancelation. As cute as the brunette was, it was really *Nikki* who'd attracted my interest the most and whom I most wanted to fuck. When I entered the salon on my appointment day, I noticed that she was also wearing a short skirt instead of her customary jeans, and when she greeted me, she pressed her mound hard against mine when we kissed.

"Have you been trying out some of your own material?" I grinned, peering down at her sexy bare legs.

"As often as I can," she smiled, motioning to the full bank of chairs. "But there's limited opportunities with the place packed from opening to closing time. We're running a little behind schedule today, so unfortunately you'll have to wait for another twenty or thirty minutes." Then she clasped my hand, passing me a metal key. "Do you want to wait in the back room? We've got a coffee maker and a more comfortable lounge for you to rest on."

"Sure," I said. "As long as you'll join me soon."

"I've got a few clients I need to check up on, then I'll come by in a few minutes. Why don't you go ahead and relax? Just don't get any ideas while you're back there. I want you to save yourself for another earth-shaking orgasm on my special chair."

"I wouldn't *think* of it," I smiled, slapping her ass as I headed to the back room.

When I opened the door, I noticed a canvas-covered couch and a few other chairs, and a single stainless-steel sink with coffee machine. The coffee smelled fresh, so I went over to the counter and poured myself a cup, then sat down peering up at the photos of the pretty models on the wall. While I stared at their professional hair styles and gorgeous faces, I wondered if they were paid models or if they were real photos of the salon's clients.

Their blank expressions suggested they were professional models, and it didn't take long for my mind to wander back to the look on the pretty brunette's face while she sat in her chair with flushed cheeks and an expression of exquisite pleasure on her face. While I peered at the different photos of the models, I snaked my right hand under my skirt and began to play with my tingling clit. Soon after, Nikki swung open the door and when she saw me rubbing my pussy, she closed it quickly and sat down beside me, taking my coffee from my other hand and placing it on the floor.

"I thought you were going to save that for *me*?" she smiled, leaning in to kiss me.

"I was looking at your pretty models on the wall and thinking back to some of the faces of the women I saw the last time I was in here. You really should update these posters with some more current photos. You'd probably attract even *more* customers if they saw how happy your clients really are when they leave this place."

"Will *you* be my first model?" Nikki purred, slipping her hand under my skirt to caress my slippery folds. "I can't think of anyone as pretty or sexy. Besides, nobody looks hotter than you when you're in throes of pleasure."

"I dunno, babe," I grinned, lifting my leg and crawling on top of her lap. "I think *you* could give some of these models a run for their money too. I bet your clients would love to see the look of ecstasy on your face when you're coming as much as they enjoy watching the other customers."

"You've already seen me orgasm watching you," she said, grinding her hips against mine. "That's good enough for me."

"It's not good enough for *me*," I said, pushing her down onto the sofa and hiking up her skirt while peering at her pretty shaved pussy. "I've been dreaming about fucking you ever since you started massaging my wet head under your sink."

"That makes *two* of us," Nikki groaned as I positioned my pussy over hers in an upright scissor position.

"Oh Nikki," I moaned, feeling her wet lips pressing against mine. "I've been dying to feel your soft flesh against me..."

"Maybe I should make some new upgrades to the salon chairs," she smiled, reaching up to caress my breasts as I began to grind my pussy against hers.

"Unless *you're* sitting on the chair underneath me, I'm pretty sure you'll never be able to replicate the experience quite like this," I grunted.

"No, I suppose not," she panted, pulling off my blouse while she unclasped my bra behind my back. I did the same, throwing her blouse on the floor beside mine, and we pulled our bodies together, pressing our bare tits against one another while we thrust our tongues into each other's mouths.

"Fuck, baby," I groaned, pressing my tingling clit against her hard mound. "You're going to ruin me for your salon chairs after this. From now on, I'm only going to want to feel your wet cunt rubbing against me."

"We might be able to arrange that," Nikki said, suddenly pushing me backwards onto the sofa and bending my knees up to my chest as she straddled my hips and began humping her sopping pussy against mine.

"Yes, Nikki," I panted, peering up at her tits swinging above me while she rocked her hips against mine. "Fuck me like you *own* me. You feel incredible."

"Even better than a vibrating plastic dildo?" she smiled, cocking an eyebrow.

"Like you said," I groaned, grabbing her tits while her clit rolled over mine. "A woman can do anything a man can do, only longer and better."

"Mmm," she said, leaning forward to press her torso against mine as she pushed my feet back even further behind my head. "And *wetter*. I want to feel you squirting all over my pussy instead of that plastic dildo. You're so fucking hot, I'm going to cum soon."

"Yes, baby," I grunted, feeling my own orgasm building up inside me like a runaway freight train. "Grind your pussy against me. I'm gonna gush all over your hot pussy."

"Oh *fuck*, Jade," Nikki wailed as she began to convulse overtop of me while breathing heavily into my mouth.

I grabbed the back of her ass with my hands and dug my nails into her cheeks while I tilted my hips forward, feeling my pussy beginning to clench open and shut. As it began pulsing in powerful contractions, I squirted my juices all over her gaping hole and exposed pucker. While my fountain washed over her ass and her lower back, we held onto each other tightly, shaking and groaning in each other's arms.

"How's *that* for a new kind of body wash?" I winked, peering into her eyes after we came down from our powerful climaxes.

"Way better than the regular massage at the sink," she smiled. "I might have to bring you back *here* next time for your styling prep from now on."

"That's *one* way to clean me up before I rest on your shaking seat," I said, feeling our combined juices rolling down over my slit and down my thighs.

Suddenly, the lunchroom door flipped open and three of Nikki's stylists peered in at the two of us still hunched over like two frogs caught humping each other.

"Can we get in on this action?" one of them said, closing the door softly behind them. "Everybody *else* in this place seems to be getting off except us. We heard you guys groaning back here and figured this might be a good time for a coffee break."

Nikki turned to look at me with a raised eyebrow, and I nodded, smiling.

"Why not?" she said, rolling off me and spreading her legs apart, inviting her colleagues to join the two of us. "It's not like the *rest* of the women won't have enough to keep themselves entertained while we amuse ourselves back here for a little while."

As the girls jumped onto the sofa and the five of us rolled around in a mangled twist of naked bodies sucking and humping each other's pussies, I couldn't help smiling at what I'd started. I had no idea when I suggested that Nikki consider upgrading her services that her salon would soon become known as the town's favorite place for lesbian orgies.

---

*R*eady *for more erotic chills and thrills? Download the exciting first story in Victoria Rush's new erotic fantasy series, The Enchanted Forest:*

Sometimes it's not just the grass that's greener on the other side...

ALSO BY VICTORIA RUSH

Wet your whistle a hundred different ways with Jade's Erotic Adventures. Browse the full collection of Victoria Rush steamy stories here:

Click to scan your favorites...

FOLLOW VICTORIA RUSH:

Want to keep informed of my latest erotic book releases? Sign up for my newsletter and receive a FREE bonus book:

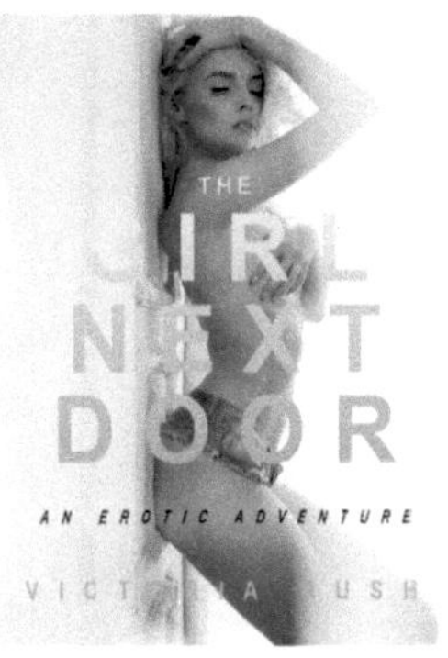

Spying on the neighbors just got a lot more interesting...